September 1940
For Emily, Julia and Cha
with love,
Amy

PLANET WAS

by
Amy Boesky

Illustrated by
Nadine Bernard Westcott

Little, Brown and Company
Boston Toronto London

For Jennifer and Rachel

Text copyright © 1990 by Amy Boesky
Illustrations copyright © 1990 by Nadine Bernard Westcott

First Edition

Library of Congress Cataloging-in-Publication Data

Boesky, Amy.
    Planet Was/by Amy Boesky: illustrated by Nadine Bernard
Westcott.
        p.   cm.
    Summary: The royal policy on Planet Was is never to change
anything, until the young Prince Hierre decides that change would be
fun and takes matters into his own hands.
    ISBN 0-316-10084-6 (lib. bdg.)
    [1. Change—Fiction. 2. Princes—Fiction. 3. Stories in rhyme.]
I. Westcott, Nadine Bernard, ill. II. Title.
PZ8.3.B59955Pl   1990   89-37433
[E]—dc20   CIP
                                                     AC

10 9 8 7 6 5 4 3 2 1

HR

Published simultaneously in Canada
by Little, Brown & Company (Canada) Limited

Printed in the United States of America

Way up high and way far back,
Behind the Seventh Zodiac,

You'll find the Planet Was, whose King —
Hierre Throdcastle Axelring —

is very short and very round
and wears a pearl and diamond crown.

Night and day he doesn't budge.
He lives on lemonade and fudge.

His idea of being King
is never to change anything.

Each King of Was is just the same:
same speech, same rules, same throne, same name.

Every King is fat and short
and nothing changes in the court.

"The Same Forever" is impressed
in gold upon the Royal Crest.

The Laws of Was are short and few:
"Never Change!" and "Nothing New!"

The parks, the streets, the houses stay
The same as they were yesterday.

Dads named Dan have sons named Dan;
Eds have Eds and Frans have Frans.

Ask why and you'll be told *Because!*
That's just the way things work on Was.

Now, King Hierre (the Fat and Short)
Has called Prince Hierre into Court.

His son at seven could have been
His royal father's royal twin:

A chubby head and tiny eyes;
A belly of enormous size,

and fudge smeared all across his face.
They sit together, Grace to Grace,

and King Hierre says, "Son, I say.
Let's do what we did yesterday!"

A thousand times *at least* to date
The Prince's answer has been "Great!"

But not today. Prince Wide-and-Short
Stares strangely 'round the little court.

"King Dad," he whispers, "can't we do
things different and try something NEW?"

"New!" King Hierre thunders. "NEW!
"For one millennium!" he booms. "For TWO

The Empire Was has stayed the same!"
Fat Prince Hierre is filled with shame.

He hangs his head. He says, "Okay.
Let's do what we did yesterday."

The King says, "Hrruumphh, that's my Hierre."
And fondly rumples up his hair.

Hierre is quiet all through chess,
Through darts, through duels,

through "Let Me Guess!"

The King is happy, but his son
Keeps wondering . . . wouldn't new be *fun*?

At ten to four King Hierre's clap
Proclaims the start of Royal Nap.

The servants snore, the nobles doze,
the whole court sleeps on mats in rows,

except the Prince, who's wide awake,
half-nibbling on some chocolate cake,

still wondering what he would do
if Was were changed to someplace new.

New homes! New roads! New names! New Kings!
New things exchanged for newer things!

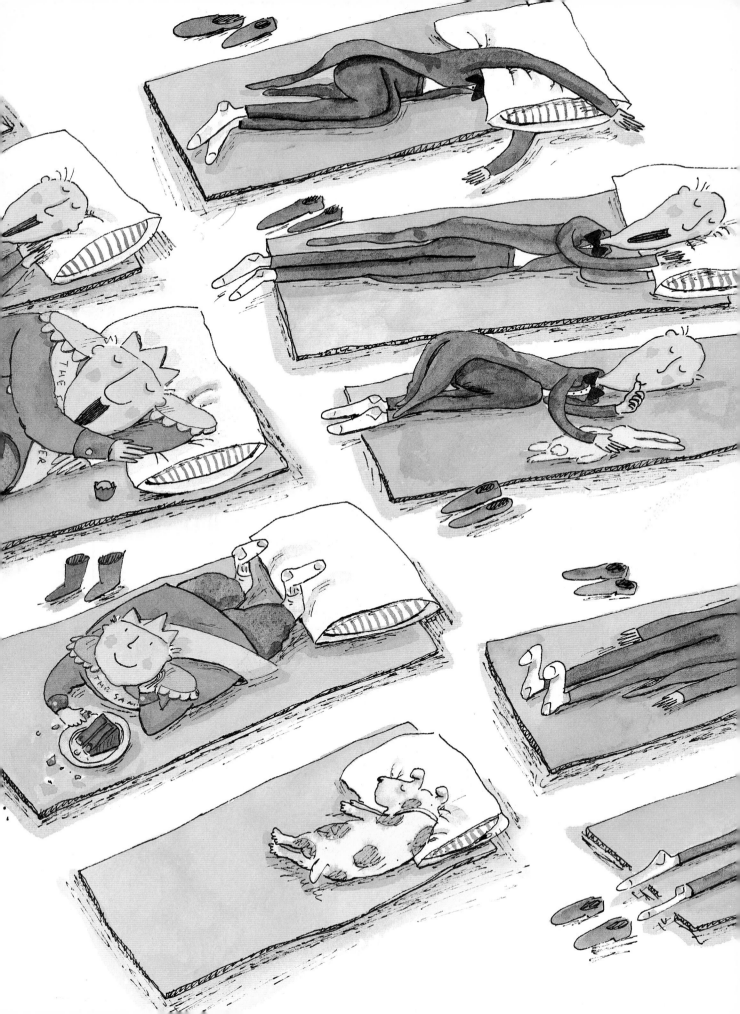

The Prince can't stand it. Up he goes
and tiptoes past the snoring rows.

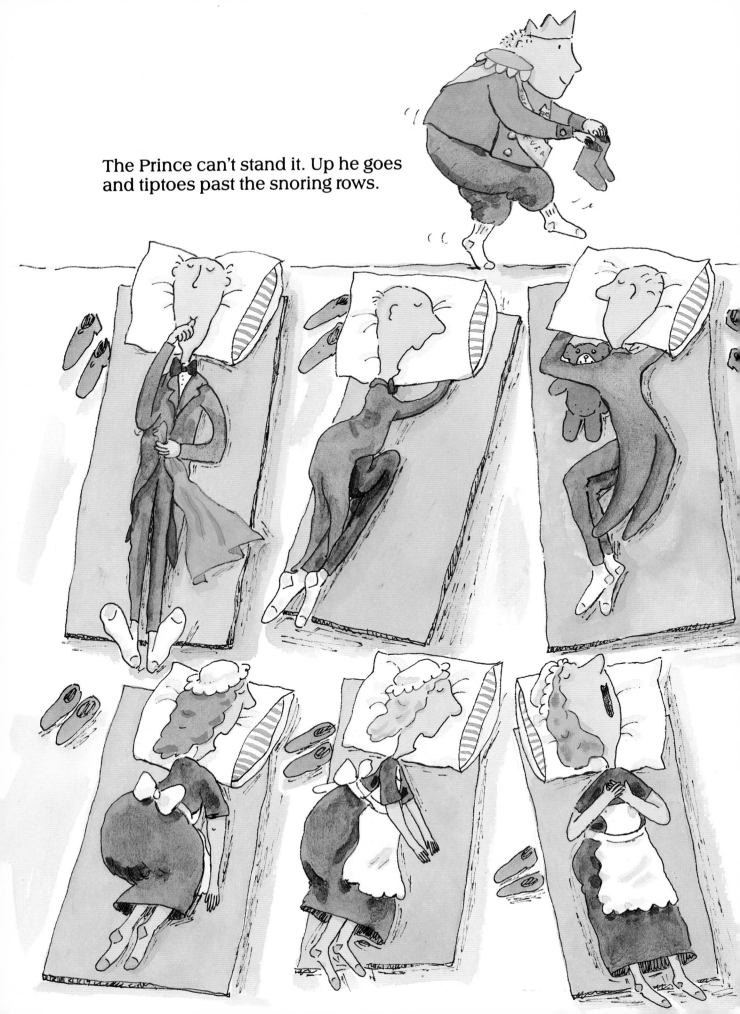

Once in his room he shuts the door
and — something never done before —

he slowly starts to rearrange.
At first he makes a tiny change:

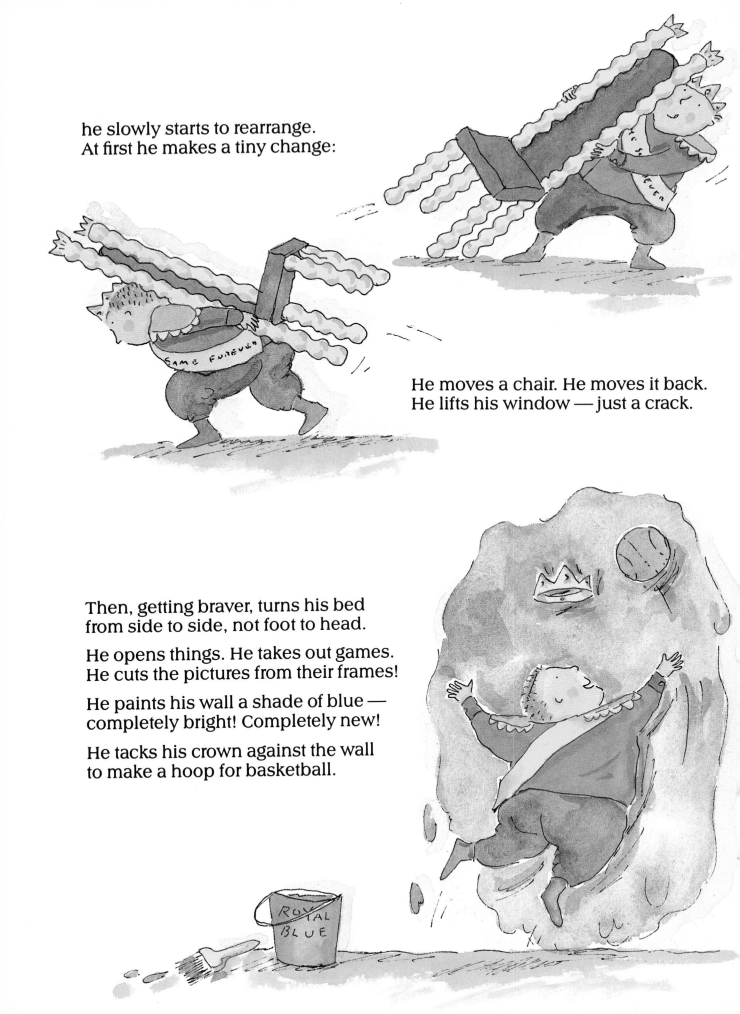

He moves a chair. He moves it back.
He lifts his window — just a crack.

Then, getting braver, turns his bed
from side to side, not foot to head.

He opens things. He takes out games.
He cuts the pictures from their frames!

He paints his wall a shade of blue —
completely bright! Completely new!

He tacks his crown against the wall
to make a hoop for basketball.

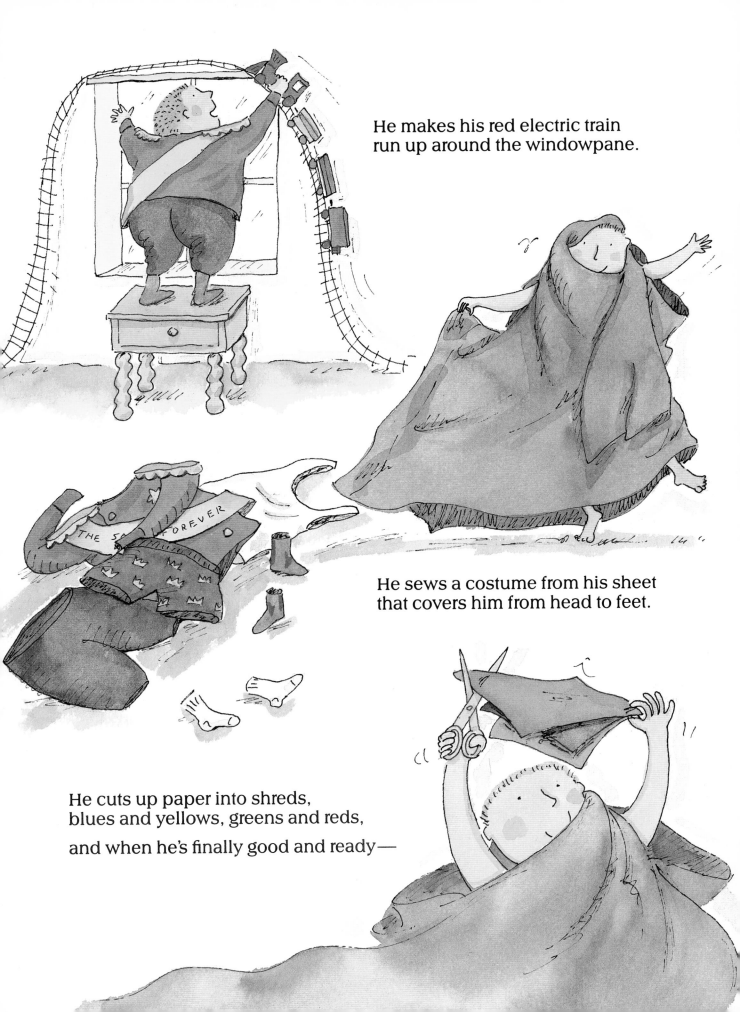

He makes his red electric train
run up around the windowpane.

He sews a costume from his sheet
that covers him from head to feet.

He cuts up paper into shreds,
blues and yellows, greens and reds,

and when he's finally good and ready—

flings them up like bright confetti!

The whole room fills with flecks of light
and Hierre dances with delight.

The room looks new — it looks like *his*.
It doesn't look like "Was" but "*Is*"!

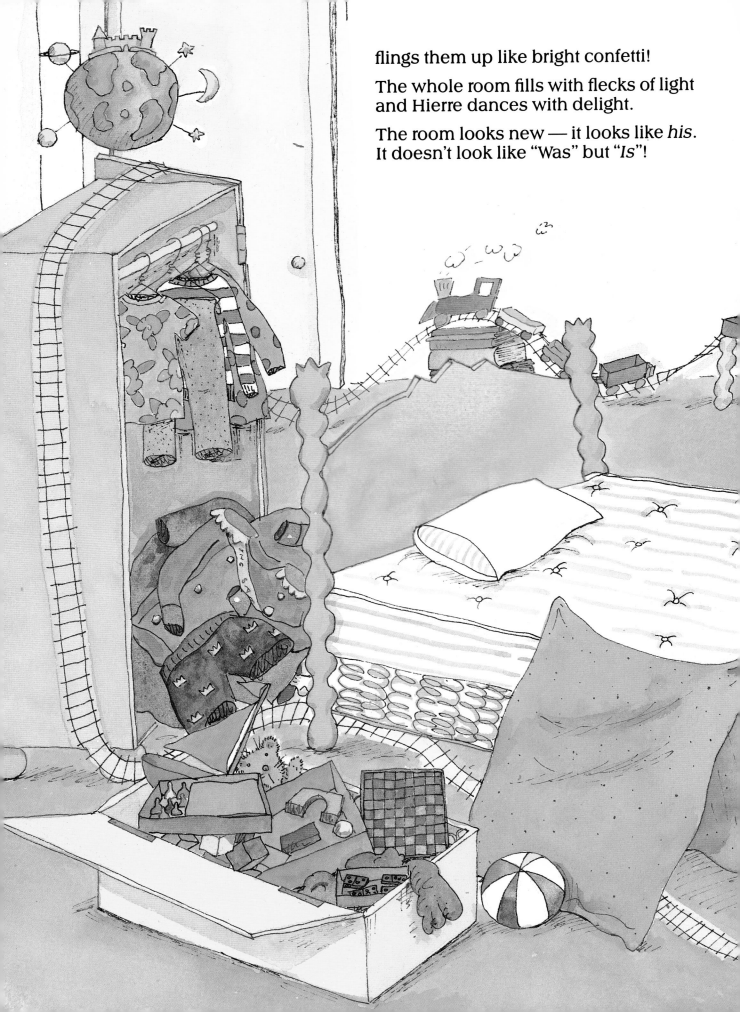

Meanwhile, H.T.A. the Fat
(the King) is stirring on his mat.

He yawns, and rubs his tiny eyes
and looks around him with surprise.

"My son!" he cries out with a yap.
"Abducted from the Royal Nap!"

He races up the castle stairs
pursued by noblemen in pairs:

Dan and Bill and Fran and Ed
all scurry to the Prince's bed

and find him there inventing toys,
each new, with a terrific noise,

a huge smile on the Prince's face
and nothing in its royal place.

"Astonishing!" the nobles cry.
King Hierre coughs. He wipes one eye.

He looks and looks and in a while —
lo and behold — he starts to smile.

"Well done!" he cries. He claps his hands.
He says the painted wall is grand.

Then H.T.A. takes off his crown,
nods his head, and looks around.

"I like it, son," he says, "I do.
I like it best because it's NEW."

And one by one the nobles grin
as out they file where they filed in.

They're off to paint their own walls blue
or, better yet, try something new!

Now dads named Dan have Bills and Eds,
Frans have Bills and Bills have Freds.

From this time on, on Planet Was
new things are welcome. Why? Because!

And right across the door that's his
Young Prince Hierre has painted: IS!